– Ch

Dad-

Here's some thoughts for those morning contemplation hours - at home or abroad.

Enjoy

Love,

Mary

NEW SUNS WILL ARISE

FROM THE JOURNALS OF HENRY DAVID THOREAU

PHOTOGRAPHY BY
John Dugdale

TEXT EDITED BY Frank Crocitto

HYPERION
NEW YORK

For my sister and brother

Kathleen and Robert

About the photographer,

John Dugdale

The photographs of John Dugdale express the still, naked beauty of life in its most pure, most ideal, and most profound forms. They reveal the sensitivity and understanding so akin to our own childhood visions that they take us aback and awaken that yearning for the kingdom of heaven that only the purest child can enter. John's transcendental photographs conjure up the words and spirit of a kindred transcendentalist, Henry David Thoreau. Here, in this amazing book, the spirits of John and Henry David dance through the many-tiered glory of the universe, a confluence that lifts us from the mundane to the transcendental fields where joy is on every flower's face.

The beauty of these images is all the more extraordinary for John's loss of sight. Due to illness, he has lost 80 percent of his eyesight and now can see only through one corner of his left eye. But since we live in a balanced universe, nothing is taken away without something else being given in its place. As it was with the ancient prophets and poets—Tiresias, the blind seer of Thebes, and Homer, the blind epic poet—John's loss of outer sight has been compensated for by the gift of insight. He sees with his mind's eye, and out of this deeper and more significant vision come the pictures you are about to see.

—Frank Crocitto

Encountering

Henry David Thoreau

(1817–1862)

To all appearances, the life of Henry David Thoreau was singularly fruitless, bringing him neither distinction nor worldly success. He was born and grew to manhood in the small Massachusetts town of Concord. Upon graduation from Harvard he worked at odd jobs—teaching, surveying, pencil-making—holding none for long. As an experiment in living he spent two years in a cabin he built in the woods beside Walden Pond. He published two books, which were mainly ignored. He fell in love once, and was rejected. Once he spent a night in jail, refusing to pay a poll tax to a state that condoned slavery. The three activities that engaged him constantly until his death at forty-four were walking, observing nature, and keeping a journal.

Through his assiduous efforts at journal-keeping, Thoreau found his vocation and his way to himself. He filled fourteen volumes with his jottings on everything under the sun. In the process he taught himself to write, creating a simple and elegant style that earned him, long after his death, literary immortality. But most important for us, his latter-day readers, as the self-appointed witness to the world of nature he extolled her beauty and intelligence profusely and with precision, and drew wonderfully striking lessons from her to illuminate human life.

To his fellow townsfolk Thoreau was a bewilderment and a disappointment, a very strange bird. He even looked like a bird—slight, wiry, with a notable beak and alert, furtive eyes. Most classed him as an idler and a dreamer. The more perceptive few, such as Emerson and Alcott, reckoned him a remarkable man who never realized his promise. The real Thoreau remained hidden from their eyes.

Thoreau reveals himself most fully in his writing. His descriptive powers, intelligence, insight, and wry Yankee humor carry the meaning and message of the man. What he has to say is even more relevant now than it was in his own time. He urges us to turn away from complexity—amassing too many things, racing about noticing nothing—to simplicity. He urges us to find time for ourselves, to go into the outdoors and find sustenance in nature. He invites us to wake up and become free men and women. Thoreau, in his life and words, epitomizes the true and original spirit of America.

At his death someone said of him: "The country knows not yet, or in the least part, how great a son it has lost . . . wherever there is knowledge, wherever there is virtue, wherever there is beauty, he will find a home."

—Frank Crocitto

Farewell, my friends, my path inclines to this side the mountain, yours to that. For a long time you have appeared further and further off to me. I see that you will at length disappear altogether. For a season my path seems lonely without you. The meadows are like barren ground. The memory of me is steadily passing away from you. My path grows narrower and steeper, and the night is approaching.

Yet I have faith that, in the definite future, new suns will arise, and new plains expand before me, and I trust that I shall therein encounter pilgrims who bear that same virtue that I recognized in you, who will be that very virtue that was you. I accept the everlasting and salutary law, which was promulgated as much that spring that I first knew you, as this that I seem to lose you.

March 28, 1856

I love very well this cloudy afternoon, so sober and favorable to reflection after so many bright ones. What if the clouds shut out the heavens, provided they concentrate my thoughts and make a more celestial heaven below!

October 12, 1851

I am surprised and enchanted often by some quality which I cannot detect. I have seen an attribute of another world and condition of things. It is a wonderful fact that I should be affected, and thus deeply and powerfully, more than by aught else in all my experience—that this fruit should be borne in me, sprung from a seed finer than the spores of fungi, floated from other atmospheres! finer than the dust caught in the sails of vessels a thousand miles from land! Here the invisible seeds settle, and spring, and bear flowers and fruits of immortal beauty.

December 11, 1855

Let a full-grown but young cock stand near you. How full of life he is, from the tip of his bill through his trembling wattles and comb and his bright eye to the extremity of his clean toes! How alert and restless, listening to every sound and watching every motion! How various his notes, from the finest and shrillest alarum as a hawk sails over, surpassing the most accomplished violinist on the short strings, to a hoarse and terrene voice or cluck! He has a word for every occasion; for the dog that rushes past, and partlet cackling in the barn. And then how, elevating himself and flapping his wings, he gathers impetus and air and launches forth that world-renowned ear-piercing strain! not a vulgar note of defiance, but the mere effervescence of life, like the bursting of a bubble in a wine cup. Is any gem so bright as his eye?

October 1, 1858

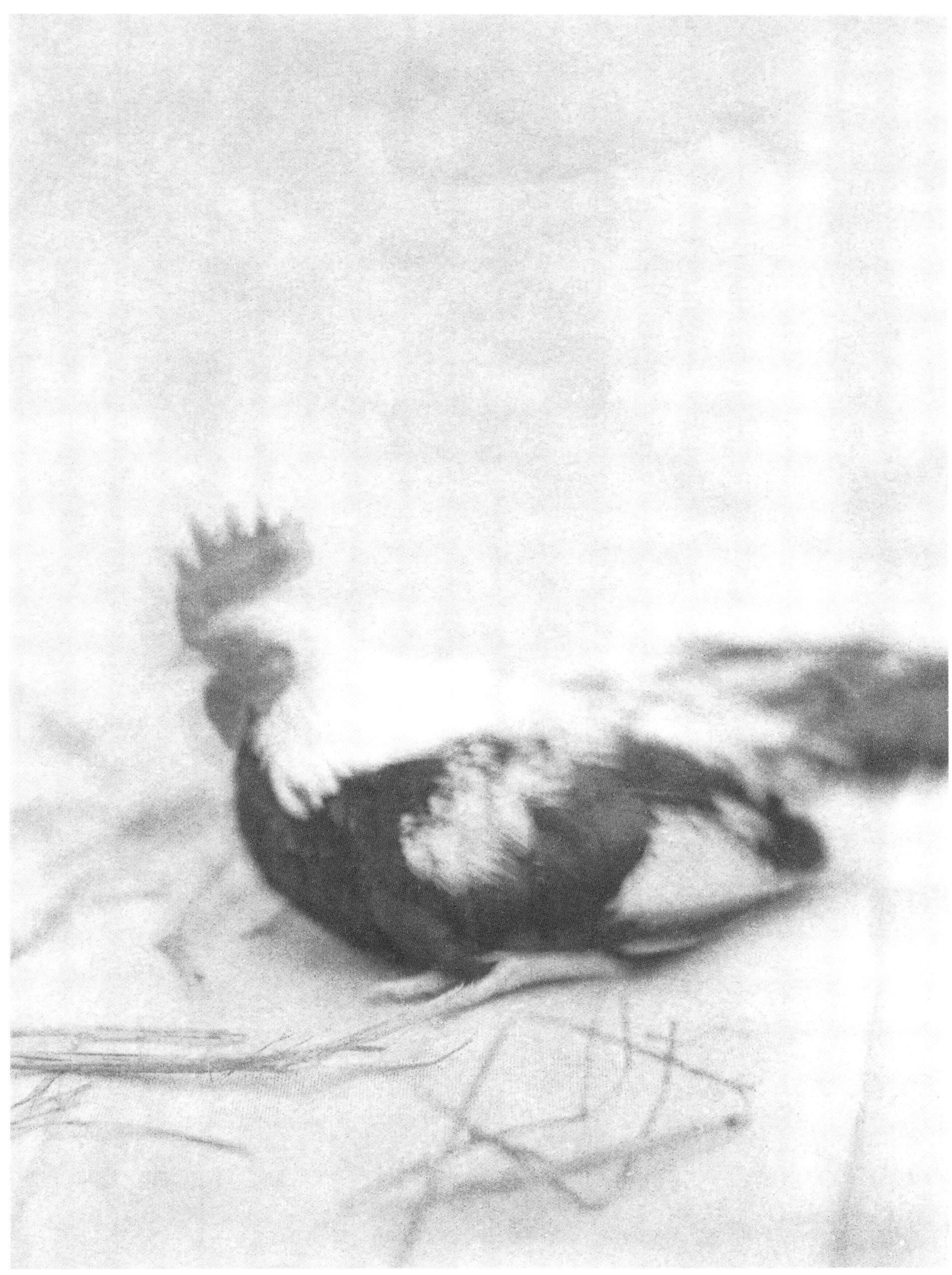

If any part of nature excites our pity, it is for ourselves we grieve, for there is eternal health and beauty. We get only transient and partial glimpses of the beauty of the world. Standing at the right angle, we are dazzled by the colors of the rainbow in colorless ice. From the right point of view, every storm and every drop in it is a rainbow. Beauty and music are not mere traits and exceptions. They are the rule and character. It is the exception that we see and hear. Then I try to discover what it was in the vision that charmed and translated me.

December 11, 1855

I know that in love there is no mistake, and that every estrangement is well founded. But my destiny is not narrowed, but if possible the broader for it. The heavens withdraw and arch themselves higher. I am sensible not only of a moral, but even a grand physical pain, such as gods may feel, about my head and breast, a certain ache and fullness. This rending of a tie, it is not my work nor thine. It is no accident that we mind; it is only the awards of fate that are affecting.

February 8, 1857

The heavens withdraw and arch themselves higher. I know of no eons, or periods, no life and death, but these meetings and separations. My life is like a stream that is suddenly dammed and has no outlet; but it rises the higher up the hills that shut it in, and will become a deep and silent lake. We have recognized each other constantly as divine, have afforded each other that opportunity to live that no other wealth or kindness can afford. Each man and woman is a veritable god or goddess. That one who does not stand so near to any man as to see the divinity in him is truly alone. I could better have the earth taken away from under my feet, than the thought of you from my mind. What if we could daguerreotype our thoughts and feelings!

February 8, 1857

May I dare as I have never done! May I purify myself anew as with fire and water, soul and body! May I gird myself to be a hunter of the beautiful, that naught escape me! May I attain to a youth never attained! I am eager to report the glory of the universe; may I be worthy to do it; to have got through with regarding human values, so as not to be distracted from regarding divine values. It is reasonable that a man should be something worthier at the end of the year than he was at the beginning.

March 15, 1852

Ah, I would not tread on a cricket in whose song is such a revelation, so soothing and cheering to my ear! Oh, keep my senses pure! And why should I speak to my friends? for how rarely is it that I am I; and are they, then, they? We will meet then, far away.

April 24, 1859

The least strain of music lifts me up above all the dust and mire of the universe. I soar or hover with clean skirts over the field of my life. It is ever life within life, in concentric spheres. The field wherein I toil or rust at any time is at the same time the field for such different kinds of life!

January 13, 1857

Love is the burden of all Nature's odes.

The marriage of the flowers spots the meadows and fringes the hedges with pearls and diamonds.

February 20, 1840

I, who cannot stay in my chamber for a single day without acquiring some rust, and when sometimes I have stolen forth for a walk at the eleventh hour of four o'clock in the afternoon, too late to redeem the day, when the shades of night were already beginning to be mingled with the daylight, have felt as if I had committed some sin to be atoned for. . . .

"Walking," an essay, 1862

Nature never makes haste; her systems revolve at an even pace. The bud swells imperceptibly, without hurry or confusion, as though the short spring days were an eternity. Why, then, should man hasten as if anything less than eternity were allotted for the least deed? The wise man is restful, never restless or impatient.

September 17, 1839

There are some things of which I cannot at once tell whether I have dreamed them or they are real; as if they were just, perchance, establishing, or else losing, a real basis in my world. This is especially the case in the early morning hours, when there is a gradual transition from dreams to waking thoughts, from illusions to actualities, as from darkness, or perchance moon and star light, to sunlight. Dreams are real, as is the light of the stars and moon, and theirs is said to be a *dreamy* light. Such early morning thoughts as I speak of occupy a debatable ground between dreams and waking thoughts. They are a sort of permanent dream in my mind. At least, until we have for some time changed our position from prostrate to erect, and commenced or faced some of the duties of the day, we cannot tell what we have dreamed from what we have actually experienced.

October 29, 1857

Perhaps what most moves us in winter is some reminiscence of far-off summer. How we leap by the side of the open brooks! What beauty in the running brooks! What life! What society! The cold is merely superficial; it is summer still at the core, far, far within.

January 12, 1855

How well behaved are cows! When they approach me reclining in the shade, from curiosity, or to receive a whisp of grass, or to share the shade, or to lick the dog held up, like a calf—though just now they ran at him to toss him—they do not obtrude. Their company is acceptable, for they can endure the longest pause; they have not got to be entertained.

July 1, 1852

Nothing must be postponed. Take time by the forelock. Now or never! You must live in the present, launch yourself on every wave, find your eternity in each moment. Fools stand on their island opportunities and look toward another land. There is no other land; there is no other life but this, or the like of this.

April 24, 1859

Live in each season as it passes; breathe the air, drink the drink, taste the fruit, and resign yourself to the influences of each. Be blown on by all the winds. Open all your pores and bathe in all the tides of Nature, in all her streams and oceans, at all seasons. Grow green with spring, yellow and ripe with autumn. For all Nature is doing her best each moment to make us well. She exists for no other end. Do not resist her.

August 23, 1853

We know men through their eyes. You might say that the eye was always original and unlike another. It is the feature of the individual, and not of the family—in twins still different. All a man's privacy is in his eye, and its expression he cannot alter more than he can alter his character. So long as we look a man in the eye, it seems to rule the other features, and make them, too, original. When I have mistaken one person for another, observing only his form, and carriage, and inferior features, the unlikeness seemed of the least consequence; but when I caught his eye, and my doubts were removed, it seemed to pervade every feature.

The eye revolves on an independent pivot which we can no more control than our own will. Its axle is the axle of the soul, as the axis of the earth is coincident with the axis of the heavens.

July 10, 1840

How enduring are our bodies, after all! The forms of our brothers and sisters, our parents and children and wives, lie still in the hills and fields round about us, not to mention those of our remoter ancestors, and the matter which composed the body of our first human father still exists under another name.

February 3, 1858

Be resolutely and faithfully what you are; be humbly what you aspire to be. Be sure you give men the best of your wares, though they be poor enough, and the gods will help you to lay up a better store for the future. Man's noblest gift to man is his sincerity, for it embraces his integrity also. Let him not dole out of himself anxiously, to suit their weaker or stronger stomachs, but make a clean gift of himself, and empty his coffers at once. I would be in society as in the landscape; in this presence of Nature there is no reserve, nor effrontery.

January 24, 1841

King James loved his old shoes best. Who does not? Indeed these new clothes are often won and worn only after a most painful birth. At first moveable prisons, oyster-shells which the tide only raises, opens, and shuts, washing in what scanty nutriment may be afloat. How many men walk over the limits, carrying their limits with them? In the stocks they stand, not without gaze of multitudes, only without rotten eggs, in torturing boots, the last wedge but one driven. Why should we be startled at death? Life is constant putting off of the mortal coil—coat, cuticle, flesh and bones, all old clothes.

1845–1847

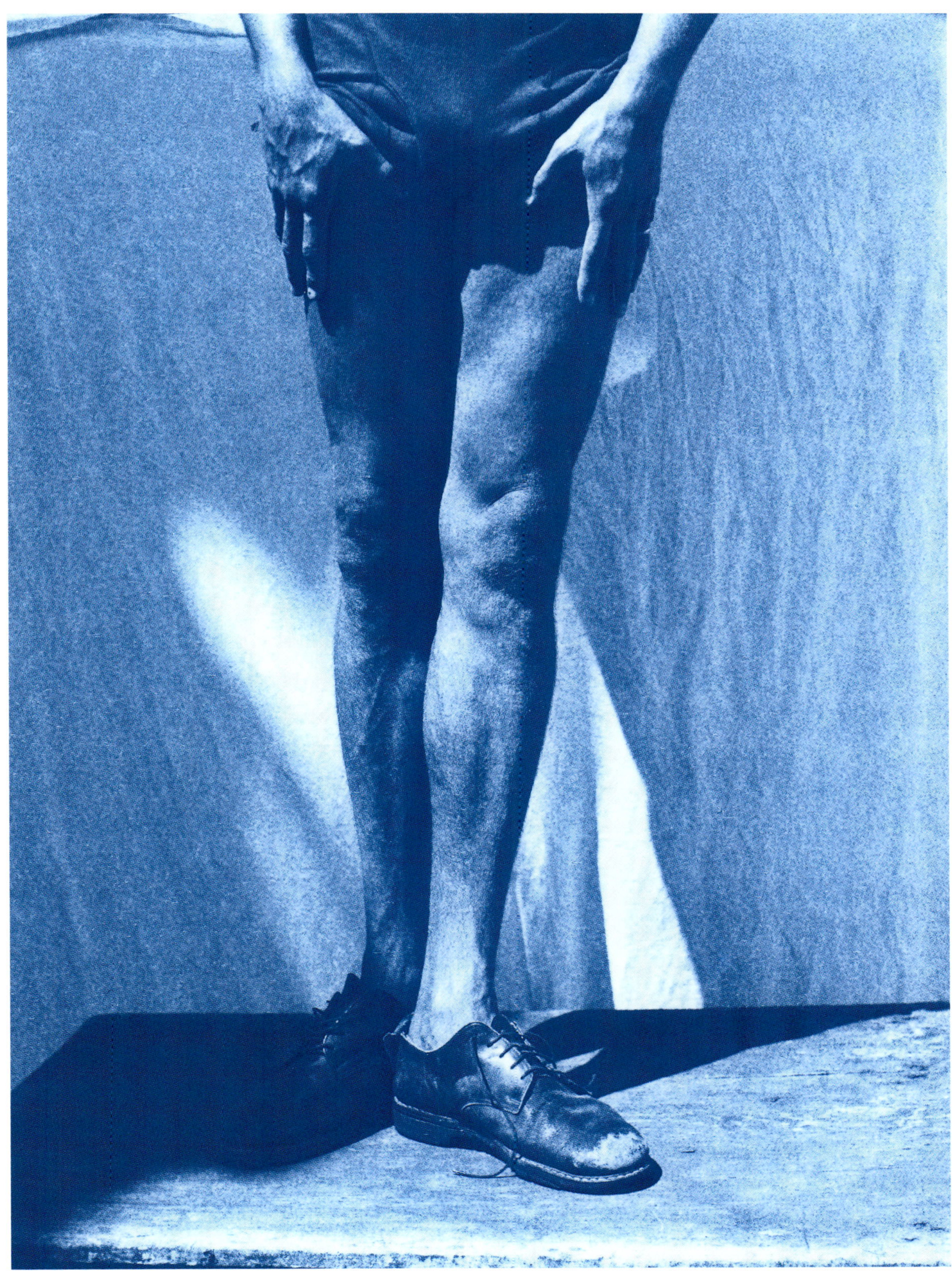

I have carried an apple in my pocket tonight—a sopsivine, they call it—till, now that I take my handkerchief out, it has got so fine a fragrance that it really seems like a friendly trick of some pleasant demon to entertain me with. It is redolent of sweet-scented orchards, of innocent, teeming harvests. I realize the existence of a goddess Pomona, and that the gods have really intended that men should feed divinely, like themselves, on their own nectar and ambrosia. They have so painted this fruit, and freighted it with such a fragrance, that it satisfies much more than an animal appetite. Grapes, peaches, berries, nuts, etc., are likewise provided for those who will sit at their sideboard. I have felt, when partaking of this inspiring diet, that my appetite was an indifferent consideration; that eating became a sacrament, a method of communion, an ecstatic exercise, a mingling of bloods, and a sitting at the communion table of the world; and so have not only quenched my thirst at the spring but the health of the universe.

July 7, 1845

The student kindles his fire, the editor packs his trunk, the sportsman loads his gun, the traveller wraps his dinner, the Irishman papers his shanty, the schoolboy peppers the plastering, the belle pins up her hair, with the printed thoughts of men. Surely he who can see so large a portion of earth's surface thus darkened with the record of human thought and experience, and feel no desire to learn to read it, is without curiosity. He who cannot read is worse than deaf and blind, is yet but half alive, is still-born.

March 10, 1856

We cannot write well or truly but what we write with gusto. The body, the senses, must conspire with the mind. Expression is the act of the whole man, that our speech may be vascular. The intellect is powerless to express thought without the aid of the heart and liver and of every member.

September 2, 1851

Often I feel that my head stands out too dry, when it should be immersed. A writer, a man writing, is the scribe of all nature; he is the corn and the grass and the atmosphere writing. It is always essential that we love to do what we are doing, do it with a heart.

September 2, 1851

Febr

Mary Fre
at no
sorey
is sick
if you think
a doctor
to get one
it bad for
no money but
be beter by the
you get
I will rite out
you mite get

Think of the art of printing, what miracles it has accomplished! Covered the very waste paper which flutters under our feet like leaves and is almost as cheap, a stuff now commonly put to the most trivial uses, with thought and poetry! The wood chopper reads the wisdom of ages recorded on the paper that holds his dinner, then lights his pipe with it. When we ask for a scrap of paper for the most trivial use, it may have the confessions of Augustine or the sonnets of Shakespeare, and we not observe it.

March 10, 1856

To be calm, to be serene! There is the calmness of the lake when there is not a breath of wind; there is the calmness of a stagnant ditch. So is it with us. Sometimes we are clarified and calmed healthily, as we never were before in our lives, not by an opiate, but by some unconscious obedience to the all-just laws, so that we become like a still lake of purest crystal and without an effort our depths are revealed to ourselves. All the world goes by us and is reflected in our deeps. Such clarity! obtained by such pure means! by simple living, by honesty of purpose. We live and rejoice.

June 22, 1851

So behave that the odor of your actions may enhance the general sweetness of the atmosphere, that, when I behold or scent a flower, I may not be reminded how inconsistent are your actions with it; for all odor is but one form of advertisement of a moral quality.

This fragrance assures me that, though all other men fall, one shall stand fast; though a pestilence sweep over the earth, it shall at least spare one man. The genius of Nature is unimpaired. Her flowers are as fair and as fragrant as ever.

June 16, 1854

Bathing is an undescribed luxury. To feel the wind blow on your body, the water flow on you and lave you, is a rare physical enjoyment this hot day.

July 9, 1852

I sometimes walk across a field with unexpected expansion and long-missed content, as if there were a field worthy of me. The usual daily boundaries of life are dispersed, and I see in what field I stand.

August 23, 1845

I see the course of my life, like some retired road, wind on without obstruction into a country maze.

February 27, 1841

If with closed ears and eyes I consult consciousness for a moment, immediately are all walls and barriers dissipated, earth rolls from under me, and I float, by the impetus derived from the earth and the system, a subjective, heavily laden thought, in the midst of an unknown and infinite sea, or else heave and swell like a vast ocean of thought, without rock or headland, where are all riddles solved, all straight lines making their two ends to meet, eternity and space gambolling familiarly through my depths.

August 13, 1838

My life was ecstasy. In youth, before I lost any of my senses, I can remember that I was all alive, and inhabited my body with inexpressible satisfaction; both its weariness and its refreshment were sweet to me. This earth was the most glorious musical instrument, and I was audience to its strains. To have such sweet impressions made on us, such ecstasies begotten of the breezes! I can remember how I was astonished. I said to myself—I said to others—"There comes into my mind such an indescribable, infinite, all-absorbing, divine, heavenly pleasure, a sense of elevation and expansion, and I have had nought to do with it. I perceive that I am dealt with by superior powers. This is a pleasure, a joy, an existence which I have not procured myself. I speak as a witness on the stand, and tell what I have perceived." The morning and the evening were sweet to me, and I led a life aloof from society of men. I wondered if a mortal had ever known what I knew. I looked in books for some recognition of a kindred experience, but, strange to say, I found none. Indeed, I was slow to discover that other men had had this experience, for it had been possible to read books and to associate with men on other grounds. The maker of me was improving me. When I detected this interference I was profoundly moved. For years I marched as to a music in comparison with which the military music of the streets is noise and discord. I was daily intoxicated, and yet no man could call me intemperate. With all your science can you tell how it is, and whence it is, that light comes into the soul?

July 16, 1851

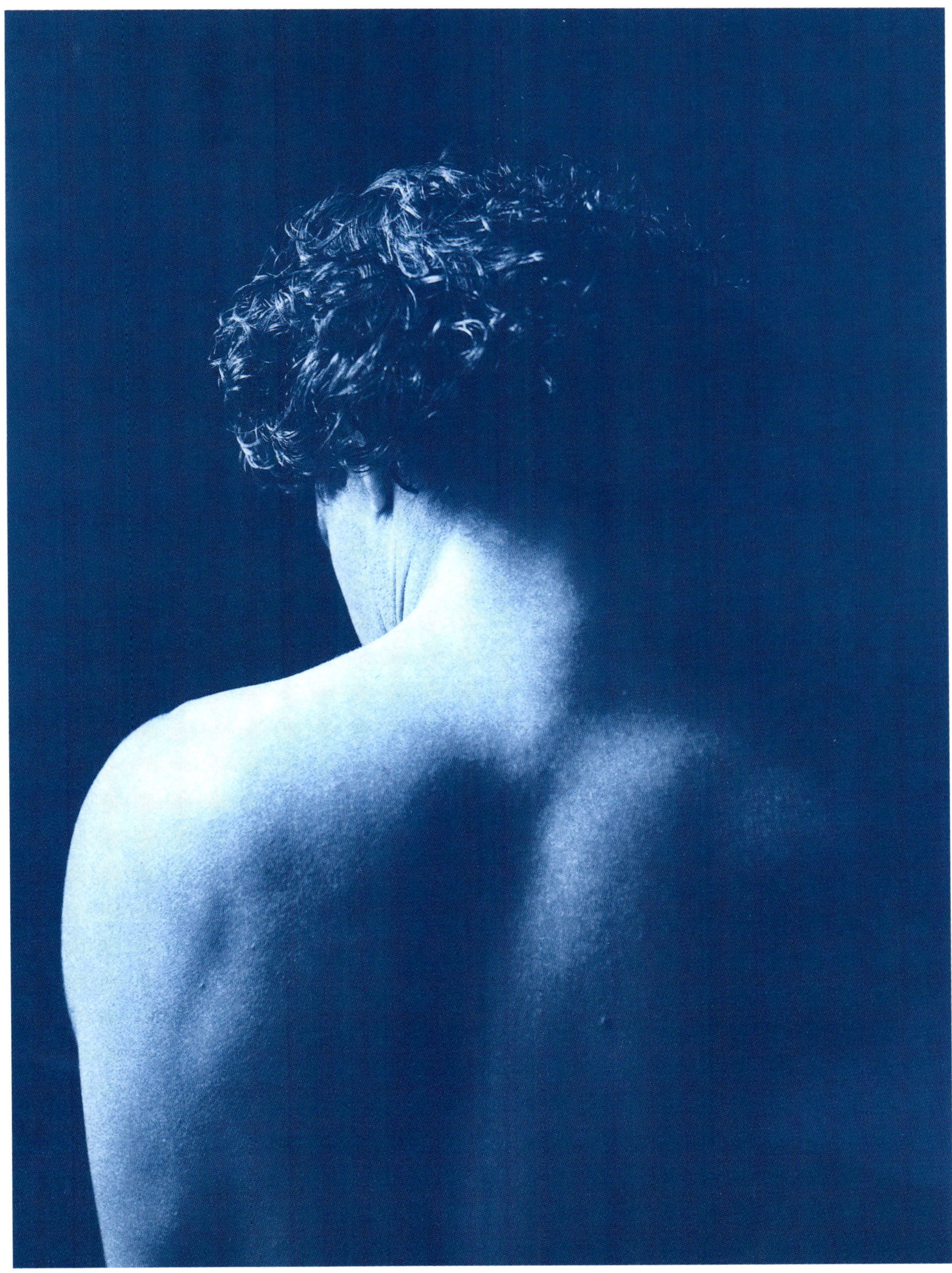

Ah! if I could so live that there should be no desultory moment in all my life! that in the trivial season, when small fruits are ripe, my fruits might be ripe also! that I could match nature always with my moods! that in each season when some part of nature especially flourishes, then a corresponding part of me may not fail to flourish! Ah, I would walk, I would sit and sleep, with natural piety! What if I could pray aloud or to myself as I went along by the brooksides a cheerful prayer like the birds! For joy I could embrace the earth; I shall delight to be buried in it. I did not despair of worthier moods, and now I have occasion to be grateful for the flood of life that is flowing over me. Nothing must be postponed.

August 17, 1851

Take time by the forelock. Now or never! You must live in the present, launch yourself on every wave, find your eternity in each moment. Fools stand on their island opportunities and look toward another land. There is no other land; there is no other life but this, or the like of this. Where the good husband man is, there is the good soil.

April 24, 1859

I find it good to be out this still, dark, mizzling afternoon; my walk or voyage is more suggestive and profitable than in bright weather. The view is contracted by the misty rain, the water is perfectly smooth, and the stillness is favorable to reflection. I am more open to impressions, more sensitive (not callused or indurated by sun and wind), as if in a chamber still. My thoughts are concentrated; I am all compact. The solitude is real, too, for the weather keeps other men at home. This mist is like a roof and walls over and around, and I walk with a domestic feeling. The sound of a wagon going over an unseen bridge is louder than ever, and so of other sounds. I am *compelled* to look at near objects. All things have a soothing effect; the very clouds and mists brood over me. My power of observation and contemplation is much increased. My attention does not wander. The world and my life are simplified.

November 7, 1855

I am from the beginning, knowing no end, no aim. No sun illumines me, for I dissolve all lesser lights in my own intense and steadier light. I am a restful kernel in the magazine of the universe.

August 13, 1838

About the literary editor,

Frank Crocitto

Besides being a zealous scholar of the great American Transcendentalists—Thoreau, Emerson, and Whitman—Frank Crocitto is a well-known poet, performer, and teacher. He has taught at Pace College and at SUNY New Paltz, and now teaches at the school he founded, Discovery Institute. Mr. Crocitto is currently in demand around the country lecturing and performing the works of Rumi and Hafiz, as well as his own recently published *Hooray for Love!*

About the photographic process

The photographs in this book were printed using a process invented in 1842. Called *cyanotype*, this process uses iron salts instead of silver for development, which gives the prints a distinctive blue hue. The cyanotypes are exposed to the ultraviolet light of the sun, rather than in a darkroom. Most of the pictures were taken in and around Ulster County, New York.

Plate titles by page

 For information address Hyperion Books for Children, 114 Fifth Avenue, New York, New York 10011-5690.

Printed in the United States of America
This book is set in 14-point Deepdene.

First edition
1 3 5 7 9 10 8 6 4 2
Library of Congress Cataloging-in-Publication Data
Thoreau, Henry David, 1817–1862.
New suns will arise : from the journals of Henry David Thoreau / photography by John Dugdale ; text edited by Frank Crocitto.—1st ed.
p. cm.
ISBN 0-7868-0539-0 (trade)
1. Thoreau, Henry David, 1817–1862—Diaries—Juvenile literature. 2. Authors, American—19th century—Diaries—Juvenile literature. [1. Thoreau, Henry David, 1817–1862—Diaries. 2. Authors, American.] I. Dugdale, John, 1960– ill. II. Crocitto, Frank. III. Title.
PS3053.A2 2000
818'.303—dc21
[B]
00-029601

John Dugdale is represented by Wessel + O'Connor, New York